I0757261

Gault, Alabama

BY

JORDAN SCHNIPER

The spirit of the times exhaled. And the world went haywire. A great humbling kicked off the Age of Sustainability and relegated the Information Age. America was already overextended. Then the Aurora Terra arrived and turned out the lights. Now ghost towns haunt the land. Once glittering cities are dark. The social contract broken in far too many areas. The old world has entered a new realm.

Exponential growth took its toll, then seized up. System down. Scale downsizing. The terms are many. Palpable societal anger over transcendent corruption and monopolistic greed. When the federal government stopped balancing budgets in the yester days, bad ideas stole from good ideas. The impact compounded as the fabric of reality began to slip. A reckoning rang the doorbell, its chime, the end of skullduggery. Now false narratives are scattered and lost in the landfills. And a whirlwind twists sour syllabic vapors in the air of tectonic change.

The golden calf of financial alchemy melted in the fires of change that the Aurora Terra brought. A film of delusion coating eyes and hearts with a frail false sense of prosperity. The solar flares and electromagnetic pulse bombs zapped the cognitive dissonance. And it all fell apart. A diluted fiat Potemkin currency edifice crumbled.

SAL ON SEA BEACH
MARINA
ENTRANCE

Dark pools of money emptied. Zombie commerce roaming caloric nothingness. Debt jubilees waging a tug of war with a daisy chain of debt defaults. A bonfire with plenty of electronic kindling as a sustainability tsunami moves over the land.

If the monetary delusion was real, where did ninety percent of the money go when the solar storm arrived? A chameleon dagger to the heart of civilization. One side of the blade was the lights going out. The other side was electronic currency vanishing on Earth as auroras ribboned the sky. Tangible cash and coin are minted, alive, and back in style.

There are even rumors of a chaos butterfly fluttering, whose viral cocoon is the human chest. The plague caterpillar airborne. Arriving as Americans returned home from Asia when the solar flares began. Citizens are advised to keep calm under medical martial law.

Foreign armies and global crime syndicate mercenaries
are on the move, coming ashore in places to test the elasticity
of national defense, probing resolve, looking for lawlessness
and weak ideologies to prey upon. The empire has ended and
the fight for the Constitution guided republic and the future
is underway. Battles await. Among the Americans, the silent
majority are armed and wait to defend.

A man from Alabama felt the strange vibrations of intuition long ago, of something like the event. Something was wrong. Something was coming. He just did not know how to process the esoteric feeling. So he traveled.

ALASKAN AIR COMMAND

He is part of Generation X, born into the greatest society that has ever existed. Now he walks into the future on a land rippled with the roots of hallowed generations. His endeavor is to survive the peril and find happiness in the great game of life.

In Gault, Alabama, resilient citizens are adapting. Self reliance and community service are the local currency for cultural acceptance. Fortitude is the mayor of the land. A goal of survival, not against odds, but based on them. Around the area, people still proudly say the old fashioned phrase, *It's a free country.* Their intent is to get out of the system and then gut it out.

Inside a hidden safe room, a shelter tucked under an antique lifting staircase, he hears the county sirens fall silent. Then he pushes the stairs up, steps out of the enclosure, and pulls the stairs down to fold them back in place. Through the windows he sees a coursing grey tornado warning sky moving north in the distance.

Down in the kitchen he loads two grocery bags with supplies from the deep pantry and walks outside. In the garden out back, crop plants glisten from the fading rain. Tomatoes, peppers, melons and corn taking on heirloom pigments from the pioneer days. A garden grows, the gardener prays, and a harvest begins its yield.

Out front, neighborhood fences are tacked with *No Trespassing* signs to ward off strangers. He loads the supplies in his truck and drives south to reunite with the woman he loves. Memories of their brief time together upon his heart. A loaded rifle leaning against the window taking a nap, and a fed pistol on the seat riding shotgun atop a grey bulletproof vest with two patches sewn on the chest.

He enters Gault, Alabama, a town of rugged individualism.
A law and order zone quarantining from the mayhem of the
spooky wastelands beyond. He rolls by the charming welcome
sign framed with circular civic organization placards. Further
on, in the parking lot of the Barter Mart, a yellow billboard with
red paint and drip lines under the letters reads,

PRIVATE EQUITY VAMPIRES NOT WELCOME
GO BACK TO YOUR MEGA CITIES

He drives along Main Street, past Alabama Denim Co. and parks in front of Merle's BBQ Pit & Market that stocks items from the nearby Zondike Farms. An old red brick chimney wicks bitternut hickory smoke up through the roof and into the air of a bluing sky. On the sidewalk corner, a weekly issue of *The Grapevine Telegraph* rests in a newspaper stand. Across the street, a baseball team loads up in a bus for a tournament up the road at Rickwood Field National Monument. The man walks in to grab some cuts of meat for his cooler, leaving room for seafood as he approaches the coast. He steps under a red herring proclamation chiseled above the entrance, *Established October 10th 1582.*

After he stocks up, chats with neighbors, and pays with green and purple tinted Liberty Dollars, he steps outside into sunshine where Bonafide Ben sits on a bench smoking a pipe in front of the barber shop. A bottle of gin set beside his right shoe, wrapped in a brown paper bag.

"How goes it young man?" His voice raspy, as if he is a distant cousin of Judge Mahlon.

"Change is upon us, sir. Glad to be back in Bama."

"That it is. We're in for the long haul. Pace yourself. Wait for it."

"What?"

"The awakening."

"What do you mean?"

"You will see soon." Ben takes a slow puff on his pipe. "So what next?"

"I'm into the wind."

"Watch out for Old Scratch."

Outside of town, a grungy man dressed in all black, with a tall hiking pack on his shoulders, and polarized sunglasses obscuring his eyes, stands in the middle of the flat road, blocking passage.

The driver stops the truck and hops out, not wanting to dabble in gore.

"Get out of the road."

"I need a ride."

"Not gonna happen."

"It needs to."

"Do you have a brother named Wayne that lives near Barstow?"

"What?" Lines of confusion etching the man's face.

"Nothing." He draws his pistol and keeps it aimed at the cracked yellow strip of highway paint. "You want to get to know me, stranger? It'll cost you your life." Watching the woods for the potential of a companion hiding to snare. He stares back at the man, not wanting to have to curl him up. "Now step aside and clear the road. I have a lady waitin' on me."

The drifter cusses, spits on the pavement, then lumbers off into the woods to lurk for the next mark. And the driver rides away and the road enters a stretch of wild forest.

Later on the coast, "Anything new?" she asks, a glow about her, a sense of peace.

"I received a postcard from the Cumberland Gap. Outlander says he's ninety percent and still healing. He's retired. And he and Mallory are now farmers working the land. They're really happy."

"Good. That's really good."

"The new American Indian members of Congress are about to be sworn in to their regional seats. They're traveling the red road. America now has indigenous seats in the Electoral College."

"It's about time. Long overdue." Her eyes narrow. "What about the fight?" She touches her fingers to the comet line scar on his neck, and then to his forearm, both gunshot wounds sustained at the Battle of Deadwood.

"The Washington Republic and Defcon Denver forces have reached Manassas. Zulu Everglades, Echo Dune, Aakicita Sioux and other Secret Eden sheriffs that survived are embedded with them. They should be able to root out the Potomac Guard in the next few weeks. And then mop up the Resistance. The coup, sedition, and treason failed."

She takes a deep breath. Nods slightly a few times with relief. Then slowly breathes out.

"Anything else?" she asks.

"I can now reconcile many years of my life. An arc has looped," he says. "And you?"

"I took a nap this afternoon and dreamt of three calico lions running through the reeds." She smiles. "Then I painted a canvas for the first time in a long time."

"Better than the dark dreams of the world. I would love to see it."

"Later. The paint is drying. And I might want to touch it up a bit."

"What color are the lions' eyes?"

"Moss green. Cobalt blue. And a cub with the heterochromatic blend of sapphire blue and fern green."

She kisses the faint purple scar on his cheek. "We found our bliss."

"Yes, we did." He looks out to the gliding waves of the sea. The echo of a restless existence circulating through his veins.

Then holds her eyes in his, admiring the copper flecks.

"We met, we parted. We reunited, we parted." He twists open the cork on a miniature tequila bottle of artisan glass, pours a tumble and takes a sip. "I mourned the fragmented time."

"It was a constant tug. I missed you. Especially late at night." He fumbles with a half a pack of American Spirit cigarettes. "It was like I couldn't take a deep enough breath and relax."

"How many a day?" she asks.

"One or two. Never on Shabbos. I just like havin' em, just in case."

She nods. "That's not so bad."

"After falling asleep in your arms, I don't know how not to. It is hard to find peace after midnight without you."

"Go on. Just talk. It's a catharsis to just say what you feel."

"I used to be really good at being alone before I met you." He pauses to take another sip of tequila. "It was like a hobby that helped me thrive as I explored. Now I just want the simple life."

"I wondered if you and I would meet again in this life." A wound of pain in his eyes from the tradeoffs along the journey. "Or have to wait until the next eternal one."

"No more. Now we have each other again. I'm not letting go."

"Me either."

"Good." She kisses him. "I'm gonna go for a swim. Wanna join me?"

"In a bit. I'll prep dinner first."

"What's on the menu?" she asks as she puts a dollop of sunscreen on her nose, followed by a stripe to cover the pale scar on her cheek.

"Grass fed steak and fresh grouper over mashed potatoes."

"That sounds perfect."

"Wanna play a game of Cowboy Chess after supper?"

She smiles. "Maybe."

He watches her walk away through the dunes and down to the water.

After getting the food started, he sits at a table with his folding typewriter and taps a question on the Corona keys.

Why were 3 books separated,
when longer ones were kept intact?

He lifts the stationery and takes scissors, cutting away all
the empty space on the page until a thin sliver with indigo ink
remains, like a ribbon. He places the words in the empty tequila
miniature and seals the line of type with the cork. A message
in a bottle to send out to sea carrying a thought. He places it
next to the Corona 3 typewriter, for later. Then he walks outside
where she is on the patio, toweling off seawater as she watches
the sunset.

Their souls were sent for this age, this generation, instead of all others. It is an act of faith to embrace it. The Constitution still lives and endures. And the national motto is still *In G-d We Trust.* Decision tree analysis to hold onto the branches of the Tree of Life during the storm and its aftermath.

That night, Levi and Naomi Wolff hold hands as they walk on the sugar sand of Seagrove Beach, below the stars, absorbing the distant arriving light. The hope of a life and an eternity together upon their hearts. A wish, a prayer. The left handed fading star of the Orion constellation flickering a mesmerizing orange hue beside yellow shining companions. A cosmic fate upon them. And life begins anew. This is the slow goodbye. A repairing of worlds awaits. It is in the tides.

www.ingramcontent.com/pod-product-compliance
Lightning Source LLC
Chambersburg PA
CBHW041732300726
48981CB00006B/323